Robots, Robots Everywhere!

By Sue Fliess

Illustrated by Bob Staake

A GOLDEN BOOK • NEW YORK

Text copyright © 2013 by Sue Fliess
Illustrations copyright © 2013 by Bob Staake
All rights reserved. Published in the United States by Golden Books, an imprint of Random House
Children's Books, a division of Random House, Inc., 1745 Broadway, New York, NY 10019.
Golden Books, A Golden Book, A Little Golden Book, the G colophon, and the distinctive gold
spine are registered trademarks of Random House, Inc.
randomhouse.com/kids
Educators and librarians, for a variety of teaching tools, visit us at RHTeachersLibrarians.com
Library of Congress Control Number: 2012939473
ISBN 978-0-449-81079-8
Printed in the United States of America
30 29 28 27 26 25 24 23 22

On the ground
and in the air,
Robots, robots
everywhere!

Up in space,

Beneath the seas,

Robots make discoveries.

Tractor robots plant and plow.

Robots even milk a cow!

Under couches, over rugs,
Vacuum robots have no plugs.

Robot dogs roll over, bark.

Can we take them to the park?

Robots spin and race and run.

Robots, robots—I want one!

Robots weld and paint and blast.

Robots build cars really fast!

Working robots drill and grind.

Rescue robots seek and find.

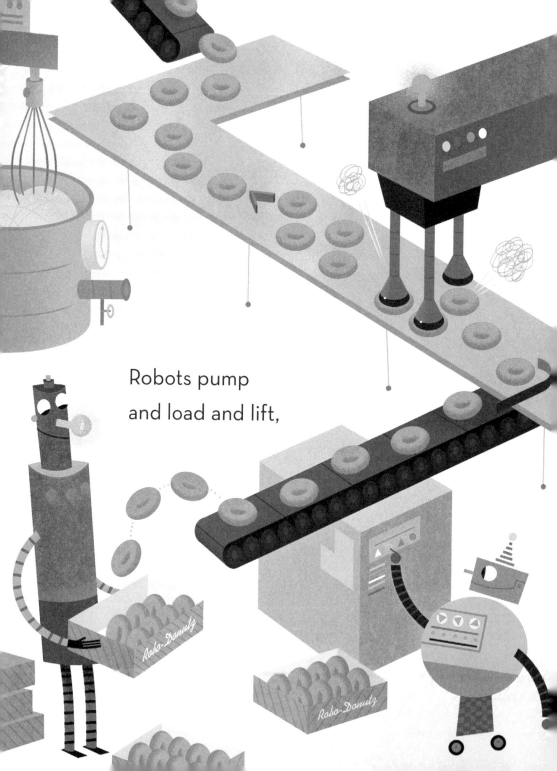

Robots pump
and load and lift,

Mix and measure,
sort and sift.

Robots beep and robots talk.
Wind them up and robots walk!

honka!
honka!

Robots made like you and me.

Robot playmates? Wait and see. . . .

Robots here and robots there,

Good night, robots everywhere!